FLYY GIRLS

NOELLE: THE MEAN GIRL

BY ASHLEY WOODFOLK

PENGUIN WORKSHOP

TO THE "MEAN" GIRLS. DARE TO BE KIND—AW

DON'T BE AFRAID TO SHOW YOURSELF
KINDNESS THE WORLD IS UNWILLING TO—ZS

PENGUIN WORKSHOP
An Imprint of Penguin Random House LLC, New York

Text copyright © 2021 by Ashwin Writing LLC. Illustrations copyright © 2021 by Penguin Random House LLC. All rights reserved. Published by Penguin Workshop, an imprint of Penguin Random House LLC, New York. PENGUIN and PENGUIN WORKSHOP are trademarks of Penguin Books Ltd, and the W colophon is a registered trademark of Penguin Random House LLC. Printed in Canada.

Visit us online at www.penguinrandomhouse.com.

Cover illustration by Zharia Shinn

Library of Congress Cataloging-in-Publication Data is available upon request.

ISBN 9780593096079 (pbk)   10 9 8 7 6 5 4 3 2 1
ISBN 9780593096086 (hc)   10 9 8 7 6 5 4 3 2 1

"We have to break up."

Noelle made the phone call from outside her apartment building just before dinner with her parents. Something had been bugging her for weeks whenever she thought of her kind, cute boyfriend, but she wasn't ready to admit what it was. She leaned against the brick and looked out at the traffic on the street. "This just isn't working anymore."

"What?" he said. "Where is this coming from? Why?"

"Travis," she said. And nothing else.

"You can't just dump me for no reason," he said. "That's so not fair."

She felt a familiar meanness rise in her, and the feeling felt like home. "Actually," she said, "I can do whatever the hell I want. And I don't want to be with you anymore. Got it?"

She hung up the phone. And as free as she felt in that moment, she also felt a little like crying.

The cello could sound angry. Especially Noelle's cello. It was what she liked most about it.

She was alone in her room, the only place she enjoyed being lately, practicing. One set of fingers moved skillfully along the neck of the big instrument and the other held the bow lightly, sliding it back and forth across the strings so quickly that her curly hair fell out of its bun and her glasses slipped down her nose. The song might not have been angry, but Noelle was, and so everything she played sounded loud and unsettled.

The school year had just started a little over a month ago, but she was already working to perfect the piece she'd play at the fall showcase. She'd mentioned the showcase at dinner earlier that night, and that had been a mistake.

"So, the fall showcase is coming up in a few weeks," Noelle had said. It was when all the students at Augusta Savage School of the Arts performed or exhibited a special piece they were excited about each year. Everyone loved the fall showcase because it was the only fun program they had all year—the only one with no grade, no real pressure; just an opportunity to show off something they were proud of, to their teachers, classmates, and families.

Before she could even finish explaining that it would be a fun night, that they didn't have to stay long, but that she really wanted them to come, her mother, an emergency room nurse, rubbed her dark eyes and said, "I'm sorry, honey, but I'll probably be pulling a double that night."

Noelle pressed her lips together and looked hopefully toward her father. She knew he had to be up at 3:00 a.m. every day to make it downtown to the construction site where he worked. He ran his hand through his spiky black hair and didn't look at her as he said he wouldn't make it either. "Won't your friends be there?" her father asked. But friends weren't the same as family.

Pierre said, "I'll come, Noey." She'd smiled at her little brother but still felt sad.

Her parents were always too busy with work to come see her play, so she didn't know why she'd expected this time to be any different. The worst part was she couldn't even be upset about them missing the showcase without feeling guilty.

Now, she played and played until the weight of the anger and guilt fell away from her tense muscles, because it was *stupid*. *She* was stupid to be upset about something like this when she knew her parents worked hard so she wouldn't have to. Her mother, Anaïs, sent nearly half of her earnings back to Noelle's grandmother in Martinique, so everything her father, Nick, made at his construction job went to their expenses. Plus, both her parents had been working extra shifts to pay for her music lessons and instruments for years. They made sure Noelle and her brother had everything they needed, and even a few things they wanted. They also let her keep whatever she made helping out at her grandparents' restaurant in Chinatown. Who was she to want more?

But she was still disappointed about *something*. And it wasn't just about her parents missing the showcase.

She knew part of her disappointment was about Travis, but she was trying not to think about how confused and hurt he'd sounded on the phone. She had a good reason to break up with him. Even though she hadn't told *him* what it was.

So Noelle played to keep her mind off him, and her family. She'd started with a mix of famous concertos she knew by heart, but as the evening turned to night she practiced original nocturnes she'd composed on her own.

Often when she played her own pieces, her deepest, most well-kept secret filled her thoughts.

She started to play more slowly, and a new, original melody filled her room. This piece—a love song—had no lyrics, but Noelle closed her eyes and thought of the only person she'd want to hear sing them if it did.

When Noelle looked down at her phone to see a text from Tobyn saying that she was in the neighborhood and asking if she could come over, it felt like Tobyn knew that Noelle had been thinking about *her*. Pierre had just left for a sleepover at a friend's house, so she had the room they shared to herself for the night. Noelle texted back, and when she let her friend in a few minutes later, her voice sounded strange and strangled when she said, "Hey, T."

Tobyn didn't notice.

"You'll never guess what Ava did to me tonight," Tobyn said, stepping inside. She went straight to Noelle's bedroom and flopped onto the bed before kicking off her shoes. They were bright yellow sneakers, and Noelle had gotten her rainbow laces. "I'll just say this," Tobyn continued, and then she sang a line from a song: *"She ain't the girl I thought she was."*

Ava was Tobyn's girlfriend. And in that moment, Noelle felt the anger and guilt reappear, and fill her up, hot and heavy.

Maybe this was the other thing stirring inside her. She knew she wasn't only mad at her parents, or upset about hurting Travis. Maybe she was also mad because Tobyn was beautiful, like the cello and its music.

But her friend was always calling someone else's name.

2

"Why are you even with her?"

The question flew out of Noelle's mouth before she could stop it.

Tobyn sat up on her elbows and pushed her fingers into her short, curly afro, and Noelle noticed the streak of blue she'd had since freshman year. The streak was perfect, so *her*, but Noelle would never tell Tobyn that.

"I know you've never liked her, Ellie. But you don't gotta say it like that."

Noelle both loved and hated when Tobyn called her Ellie. She loved it because it made her feel like she was special to Tobyn. But Noelle hated it for the same reason, because she knew she really wasn't—not in the way she wanted to be.

"I just mean," Noelle said, trying to backtrack and push away her impatience, "that you complain about her all the time. She isn't good to you. So I don't get why you're with her if you're so unhappy."

Tobyn frowned. "I didn't say I was unhappy. I didn't even tell you what happened yet," she said.

"So tell me," Noelle replied. She started putting away her cello so she didn't have to look at Tobyn while she talked.

"So, we were at her house making out, right?"

Noelle felt grateful to be looking down at her cello case, taking too long to fasten the clamps.

"Uh-huh," she muttered, trying to ignore the pain that filled her chest when she thought about Tobyn kissing anyone.

"And when her mom knocks on her bedroom door, she goes to push me off of her, but my earring got snagged in one of her braids."

Noelle knew she couldn't look at her cello for the whole story, so she stood up and crossed her room to open her window. She imagined how close two humans would need to be for an earring to get stuck in a braid on someone else's head.

"Ouch," Noelle said.

"I know," Tobyn agreed. "So I'm like, 'Wait a second, I'm stuck.' But Ava keeps pushing me."

"I thought her parents were cool with you two dating?" Noelle asked. She needed to find something else to do to keep her hands and eyes busy, so she picked up Tobyn's shoes and put them together by the end of her bed.

"Oh she's out and they're definitely cool with us going out, but we're not allowed to like, hook up whenever we want. The same way your parents would flip if you had a boy in here and they caught you kissing."

Noelle nodded, thinking about Travis. She liked kissing him, and had done it often enough in this room while they were together. But part of the reason she'd broken things off with him was that sometimes, especially lately, she thought about kissing other people, too.

"So anyway," Tobyn continued, "she kept pushing, and it was hurting me more than her, you know? The doorknob started to turn and I was still saying, 'Ava, gimme a second, I can just take my earring off,' when the snag came loose and I fell on the floor."

Tobyn reached for Noelle's arm and said, "Will you sit down for a second?"

Noelle swallowed hard at Tobyn's touch. It made her blush. But she played it off. She pulled her arm away and rolled her eyes, sat down, and looked at her friend. "I don't know why I have to look at you to listen," she said. Tobyn just continued the story.

"So her mom walks in, sees me on the floor, and I pretend I'm tying my shoe. My earring is dangling from the end of Ava's braid but her mom doesn't notice and just asks if I'm staying for dinner."

Tobyn smiled to herself. "It's actually kinda funny when I think about it now, but I was pissed then. So I told her mom no, I wouldn't be staying. And once she left I said to Ava, *'What the hell?,'* yanked my earring out of her hair, and left." Tobyn leaned closer to Noelle and pointed to her earlobe. It was a little torn and a tiny bead of blood sat right near her piercing.

"Jesus," Noelle said, and reached out to touch it. "Does it hurt?"

"Duh," Tobyn said. "And look, I get why she didn't want to get caught but . . . something else happened tonight, too."

"What?" Noelle asked. She watched Tobyn's eyes as they traveled all around her room. Her friend looked sad. "Tobyn. What?"

"When we were kissing, it felt different for some reason." Tobyn squeezed her hands together and Noelle stayed quiet. "I don't know if she loves me anymore."

Noelle had barely been holding it together having to sit so close to Tobyn, having to hear her complain about her girlfriend. But the worst of it was the hope that rose up inside her as Tobyn told this last part of her story.

The hope that if Ava didn't love Tobyn anymore, maybe there would be room for Tobyn to love . . . someone new. It reminded Noelle too much of hoping her parents would come see her play, and she hated hoping for things that might never, ever happen.

The anger returned again, but this time, instead of feeling hot, Noelle's whole body went cold.

She imagined the hope was a candle. She blew out the flame.

"God you're so dramatic, Tobyn," Noelle said. And she knew her voice sounded mean. "She ripped your earlobe open. You're literally sitting here bleeding, and you fight with her all the time. Don't be dumb. Just dump her if you think she hates you so much."

Tobyn's eyes turned hard. She stood up and grabbed her shoes, but she didn't even put them on. "You're such a bitch sometimes, Noelle. I don't know why I even came here. I don't know what your problem is."

Tobyn slammed the bedroom door when she left and Noelle didn't move. She just sat there, imagining Tobyn on the floor in Ava's bedroom, wearing one earring, pretending to tie the rainbow laces in her yellow shoes.

Noelle hadn't been looking forward to school on Monday, especially orchestra class. She knew she'd have to see Travis. And as soon as she walked in, there he sat with his saxophone, glaring at her. She nodded at him, but he looked away from her immediately.

She was also dreading orchestra because she hadn't spent as much time practicing as she should have. Between the breakup, perfecting her nocturne, and adding to the new ballad, she just hadn't had time. She was first chair, so whenever she didn't practice enough or missed a note, Ms. Porter, the instructor, noticed.

As Noelle expected, she was not prepared. As Ms. Porter directed the class to play a symphony, Noelle's lack of practice combined with Travis's heated looks, and she stumbled through it several times.

"Noelle," Ms. Porter said, pulling her aside after class. "I really need you to be the example for the rest of the string section, and really the rest of the orchestra. If first chair is too much responsibility . . ."

"It isn't, Ms. Porter. I promise." Noelle couldn't lose first chair; she'd worked too hard for too long to get it. She knew she'd have to do better.

When she stepped out of class, Travis was waiting for her in the hall.

"So," he said.

"So what?" she said.

"I want to know why."

Noelle sighed. "I can't do this right now," she muttered. And she left him there, alone in the hallway.

At home that night, when Pierre stepped into their bedroom, Noelle saw that his jeans were ripped and his knee was bleeding. His shirt was also all grass-stained and dirty.

"What happened to you?" Noelle asked her brother.

"Nothing," he said.

"You know you're a bad liar," Noelle replied.

Pierre paid her no attention, grabbed a change of clothes, and went back down the hall to the bathroom.

He returned to their room in a clean T-shirt and shorts, with a Band-Aid over his knee. When he started playing a video game in bed, he seemed fine. But Noelle watched her brother closely for the rest of the evening anyway.

3

"So, I hope graffiti isn't your prank idea," Micah said.

Noelle told the girls she had an idea for their senior prank after Micah had taken them all to a bridge in East Harlem that was covered on its underside with giant portraits, tiny tags, and life-sized memorial art. Even though Micah's brother had painted there sometimes in the year before he'd passed away, Noelle knew Micah didn't have it in her to follow in his footsteps.

Lux laughed and said, "I'm probably the only one with the balls to do that."

Both Tobyn and Noelle were offended. They shouted, "Hey!" at the same time. They looked at each other, but instantly looked away.

The roof of Micah's apartment building was the girls' favorite after-school hangout. Noelle dragged a lawn chair closer to where her friends were sitting, but even the loud scraping noise it made didn't make Tobyn look at her. They hadn't spoken since the other night in Noelle's bedroom, when she'd told Tobyn she should break up with Ava.

"I'd say my idea is graffiti adjacent," Noelle started, settling into the chair. A cool October breeze floated around them. "Similar, but less . . . permanent."

"Since our first ever prank was releasing the butterflies, I think our last one should sort of call back to that." The butterflies had been a part of the reason they were called Flyy

Girls, and Noelle thought they should honor their name in what might be their final prank. "I think we should wrap cellophane around the flagpoles on either side of the school doors, the door handles, the hinges, all of it, so it's impossible to enter the school without cutting through it all. Then we can spray-paint the plastic wrap any way we want. I thought it would be cool to just cover the whole thing in huge, colorful butterflies." As Noelle talked, she couldn't help but glance in Tobyn's direction. But Tobyn looked everywhere except at her.

Noelle pulled up a video on her phone of people who had done something similar so they could see what it might look like.

"Oh, I love this idea," Lux said. Micah asked a ton of questions, but Noelle had answers for everything. She'd thought it all out. "The only problem is how to get the spray paint.

Since none of us are eighteen, we can't just go buy it." She glanced at Tobyn again, who was the only one of them who had an older sibling.

"Could Devyn help?" Noelle asked. But Tobyn shook her head. "She's always on me about how I need to be the 'good one' for Mom. She'd never go for helping me with something like this."

"I could probably get us fake IDs," Lux said. But Noelle frowned. "Nah. If we got caught with that, you could get into real trouble," she said. "I don't think it's worth it."

They tossed around a few other ideas for how they might pull it off, but none of them seemed all that great.

"Should we even risk it?" That was the only question Tobyn had. "Because this is a little more dangerous than our other pranks. And what if the paint accidentally got on something other than the plastic? That's vandalism." Noelle looked at Lux and Micah.

Lux nodded without hesitation. "It's too good not to," she said. Micah agreed and added, "I'm nervous, but it's kinda brilliant. You scared, T?"

Tobyn rolled her eyes. "Of course *I'm* not scared. I'm going to be singing and traveling the world next year. I just don't want any of *you* to get caught. It's senior year. I don't want this to like, affect your college stuff, you know?"

Noelle had been thinking about college more and more lately, and the Manhattan School of Music was where she wanted to go. It scared her to think about leaving everything and everyone she knew behind, so she decided she wasn't going to. She hoped wherever Tobyn landed wouldn't be too far away, but she knew her friend would follow music wherever it took her.

"Colleges won't give a crap about a dumb prank. Plus, everyone in America does a prank their senior year. It's like, a rite of passage," Noelle promised.

"True," Tobyn allowed. "But what if this one prank makes Principal Powell realize that we did all the other ones, too?"

"I don't think he's smart enough to put all that together. Plus, our pranks are harmless. And as long as we're careful, this one will be, too."

They talked about other things for a while before Tobyn told Micah and Lux the story about Ava. She didn't mention the part about Ava not loving her anymore, and Noelle wondered why. Noelle stayed out of it, though, and pretended to text someone, even though pretty much everyone she ever messaged was right here on the roof.

"I just don't know what to do about her,"

Tobyn said. Lux told her to trust her gut. "The only person who knows how she makes you feel is you."

Micah told her to wait. "Just wait and see. You change your mind like every other day, Tobes. Just give it a minute."

Noelle was still looking at her phone, but she could feel Tobyn's eyes on her for the first time all evening.

"Noelle told me to dump her," Tobyn said, and Lux laughed. Noelle looked up, pushed her glasses farther back on her nose, and shrugged.

"Do whatever you want, T," Noelle said. She didn't mean it to sound like she didn't care, but that's the way it came out. She couldn't take it back.

Tobyn looked at Noelle, then asked her another question about the prank and college and the possibility of it all ending in disaster.

Noelle let out an annoyed sigh.

"Ugh. If you're so worried, we can do it without you."

Tobyn screwed up her face and pressed her lips together so tightly that Noelle thought she might cry.

"I'm just trying to look out for you," Tobyn said, and her voice sounded heavy, like she didn't think Noelle would do the same for her.

"I don't need you to," Noelle replied.

"Jesus, Ellie. I'm just asking—"

"Stop calling me that."

"Guys, don't fight," Micah pleaded.

Lux looked confused and said, "Yeah. What is with you two today?"

"Nothing," both Noelle and Tobyn said.

"I gotta go anyway," Noelle added. "I'll see you guys later."

4

Back at home, Noelle grabbed the mail from the mailbox before heading up to the apartment. There were a few bills, one with red lettering that looked like they'd missed a payment, and a letter her grandmother had sent her from Martinique. She and her Granna Esther had been something like pen pals for as long as Noelle could remember, and over time, Noelle found she could write down more true things than she could ever say out loud. *Don't tell Mama*, she'd written to Granna Esther so many times, before telling her grandmother secrets no one else knew. Noelle lifted the letter to her nose and sniffed. It smelled like the rosewater soap Granna Esther always used. She couldn't smell roses without thinking about her grandmother's soft, dark skin.

Noelle hadn't been back to Martinique since middle school, but she remembered everything about it: the tall palm trees and turquoise water, the way the air felt like a solid thing because it was so humid. There were green mountains and colorful houses and these small, spotted lizards that were everywhere the way squirrels were in New York. She missed the island and her family there. Especially Granna Esther.

The last time Noelle visited Martinique, she was helping Granna Esther clean fish on her front porch. Noelle told her grandmother about all of her twelve-year-old drama. It just slipped out that she and her best friend had accidentally broken her mother's locket, then figured out, all on their own, how to fix it.

Noelle knew Mama would have scolded her and then demanded to know what had happened. But Granna just listened and told her she was "very clever." Noelle knew Granna believed in her—she believed that Noelle was good and smart and kind, even though there were lots of moments when she wasn't. And there was something about the faith Granna always had in her, even then, that made Noelle know she could be trusted.

Now, Noelle sat down in the kitchen and read Granna Esther's letter. Her grandmother talked about her aunt, Tantie Oceane, and how sick she was. She wrote that the rains came to the island because it was hurricane season, and that she had a leaking roof. She wrote about a book she was reading and said that she hoped it wouldn't end. *I miss you, Little One,* her grandmother had written. *How are your friends? And school? It's your last year and I can't believe it. Tell me everything.*

Noelle pulled out a notebook from her nightstand drawer and started writing out her response.

⁂

October 14

Bonjou Granna Esther,

I miss you, too. I'm sad summer is over, but school is okay so far. Teachers haven't been too annoying yet, but my orchestra teacher is stressing me out a little. She's worried I'm not taking first chair seriously, but I swear I am! There's a fall showcase coming up next month and I'm going to play a song I composed, the one I told you about? Maybe we can find time for a video call so I can play it for you.

Mama and Dad can't come to the showcase and I'm pretty annoyed about it. Like, I know they have to work but sometimes I wish they cared about my music the way you do.

Tell Tantie Oceane that I hope she feels better soon. I'm going to include my (other) grandma's recipe for tomato egg drop soup. Nǎinai always makes it for me when I'm sick.

I'm worried about Pierre. He's still fighting with kids at school and I'm afraid he's going to get kicked out or worse. Mama and Dad just get pissed and yell at him. Maybe you can call him? He might listen to you.

There's something else I wanted to tell you, Granna, but I've been kinda scared. It's a secret, so you can't tell Mama.

I have a crush on someone . . . a girl. And no one knows this, but that's why Travis and I broke up. The girl is my friend Tobyn; remember me telling you about her? She's beautiful and kind and she can sing. But since she's my friend, I don't want to ruin everything by telling her the truth. At the same time, I'm worried if I don't tell her I'll ruin

*everything anyway. We've already been
fighting a lot.*

What do you think I should do?

As she finished the letter and tucked it into an envelope, Noelle heard someone enter the apartment. It sounded like they were crying.

She put the envelope on the kitchen table and looked down the hall. She saw Pierre there, dropping his backpack on the floor, rubbing at his face with his sleeve. His shirt was torn and his eye looked like it might be swelling.

"Pierre, what the hell happ—"

"I'm fine," he said immediately. He went into their room and slammed the door shut.

The next day Noelle skipped last period.

She didn't know much about what was going on with Pierre but after yesterday it occurred to her that the fights he got into might be happening on his way home from school. When he showed up at the apartment with scratches and bruises, refusing to tell anyone what had happened, the injuries were always fresh. Noelle wanted to test her theory.

But on her way out of a back exit, she bumped right into Tobyn.

"Oh hey," Tobyn said. "Why aren't you in class?"

Noelle didn't want to tell her. But trying to come up with a lie might take longer than just telling the truth. And she needed to get out of there quickly. She whispered, "I'm skipping."

"Oh," Tobyn said. She stepped closer to Noelle and lowered her voice. "Well look,

I don't really know what's going on with us, but can we squash it? I . . . miss you."

She and Noelle had been in their non-fight for almost a week, and though Noelle wouldn't admit it out loud, she missed Tobyn, too.

Noelle shrugged, not wanting to give in so easily. But when Tobyn looked hurt, something inside Noelle caved. She hated when Tobyn felt sad, and she hated it more when it was her fault. She couldn't seem to stop hurting her feelings, even by accident, but right now, Noelle knew she could fix things.

So she sighed and said, "Don't look so upset. We're cool."

"Are you sure?" Tobyn said.

Noelle nodded.

Tobyn hugged her and said, "Great. I need to get out of here, too. Forgot to do Ms. Garrett's homework. Mind if I come with you?"

Noelle usually had no trouble holding grudges, but lately, it was nearly impossible for her to stay mad at Tobyn.

"Fine. We have to pick up my brother first, though," Noelle told her.

"Oh yay!" Tobyn replied. "It's been too long since I've seen Lil P."

They walked the dozen or so blocks between Savage School of the Arts and Langston Hughes Middle School in relative quiet. Noelle felt nervous and was even more aware of her feelings than usual with Tobyn so close.

They got to Pierre's school right before the last bell. As the kids poured out of the wide double doors, Noelle looked for Pierre's brown skin and wild, dark hair in the crowd. She found him, spotted his green, spiky backpack, and looped her finger through his shoulder strap before he saw her.

"Hey, Big Head," she said. She threw her arm over his shoulder. He smiled up at her.

"What are you guys doing here?" he asked. He gave Tobyn a high five.

"What's going on, lil man?" Tobyn said.

"Nothing," he answered. His eyes looked bright.

"Good day?" Noelle asked.

"It was okay."

Noelle didn't answer Pierre's question about why they'd come. Instead, she said, "Wanna get a doughnut?"

"Sure!" Pierre said. He bounced ahead of them and started talking about his day. His seventh-grade adventures were cute. When Tobyn looped her arm through Noelle's, she tried to focus on what her brother was saying instead of how warm her face felt whenever Tobyn touched her.

They were almost at the doughnut shop when Noelle noticed that Pierre's bouncy walk had slowed, and he kept looking behind them. Noelle followed his gaze and her eyes landed on two boys who looked like they were older than Pierre, but younger than her. She stared at them.

"Who are those guys?" she asked Pierre.

"No one," Pierre said. Tobyn looked back at them, too.

"P," Noelle said again. "Look at me. Are they the punks who've been beating you up?"

She heard her mistake as soon as it passed her lips.

Pierre's whole body went stiff. His eyes got mean. "They don't 'beat me up.' We fight. Because they say dumb things to me until I have to hit them."

"What do they say to you?" Tobyn asked.

She eyed the boys again, and Noelle thought Tobyn looked as mad as she felt.

"Dumb stuff. Ever since I had that panic attack at school."

Oh. Noelle thought, and she could imagine what they'd said. They probably called him a freak or a spaz. They might imitate the way his breath would have come too quickly or the way he'd covered his ears and cried.

"Little jerks," Tobyn said.

Noelle rounded on the boys. She wanted to murder them.

"Noey, don't," Pierre said.

"Why not?" Noelle asked. But Pierre held her arm tight and the boys laughed at her. Then Tobyn said to one of them, "Hey, I know your brother. Which means, I know where you live. I have no problem coming to your apartment and telling your mother that I saw you out here being a little shithead." The boys stopped laughing. "She really know your brother?" one asked the other. He shrugged. They looked at each other, looked at Pierre with what Noelle thought might be a threat in their eyes, and then they ran away.

Pierre said, "Do you really know his brother?"

"Nah," Tobyn said. "I took a chance that he even had one."

Pierre cracked up, but Noelle still looked pissed.

At the doughnut shop, Tobyn asked Pierre what flavor he wanted, and got a lemon poppyseed one for herself. "Noelle," Tobyn said, "you want Boston crème?"

Noelle's nostrils flared.

"Pierre, do those boys follow you home every day?"

Her brother had already bitten into his

doughnut. "Not every day," he said around the food in his mouth. "But sometimes, yeah."

"Are they who you've been fighting with the last couple of weeks?"

"Do we have to talk about this?" he said. "I just want to enjoy this doughnut in peace. Want a bite?"

"No," Noelle said. Pierre rolled his eyes, and Noelle said, "You better cut that out right now."

"You're not my mother," Pierre said. Before Noelle could say anything else, Tobyn cut in.

"Hey," she said to Pierre. "We'll be right back." Tobyn took Noelle's elbow and steered her outside.

Once the door shut behind them, Tobyn frowned at Noelle.

"Don't be a dick to Pierre just because you're mad," Tobyn said. Noelle crossed her arms and rolled her eyes.

"I'm not," Noelle insisted.

"You *are*. You always do this, Ellie." Tobyn looked a little embarrassed, and Noelle remembered telling her not to call her by that nickname. "I mean, *Noelle*. You did the same thing to me last week, even though I *still* don't know what you were so mad about." Tobyn nibbled on her lip and Noelle knew Tobyn only did that when she was hurt and trying to hide it.

Noelle couldn't help but remember, in that moment, how Tobyn had looked on the first day of eighth grade. Just like Lux had been the new girl last year, Tobyn had been new back then. But Tobyn hadn't been nervous at all. She was just ready to be friends with everyone.

Micah wanted to talk to her, but Noelle felt hesitant. Noelle reminded Micah that thirteen-year-old girls could be ruthless. The two of them had become friends when Noelle saved Micah from a bully the year before. "But Tobyn's nice," Micah insisted. "I talked to her this morning."

"That's why I'm worried," Noelle said. Tobyn seemed a little *too* nice. Noelle didn't trust her, so she did what she'd always done to test loyalty: She whispered a few harsh words to Tobyn about another girl in their grade. If Tobyn would gossip about someone she didn't know, that would show she wasn't as sweet as everyone thought. But Tobyn didn't smile, and she didn't join in. She said, "What'd that girl ever do to you?" Noelle was pleasantly surprised that Tobyn stood up to her instead of laughing.

Tobyn's niceness was actually kindness, and it was then that Noelle learned the difference. And lately it was that kindness that made Noelle want to be close to Tobyn in a way she never had wanted to be before.

Noelle could tell Tobyn why she'd gotten so mad at her the other day now. She could tell her about Travis and reveal the truth about everything. But Tobyn was too soft, too sweet to love her—a girl with so many sharp edges.

"You're right," Noelle said. "I'm sorry." Tobyn nodded, but something still felt off between them.

"Okay. Call me later?"

Noelle uncrossed her arms. "Okay," she said.

"I got you the Boston crème anyway," Tobyn said, handing Noelle the paper bag she was holding. Then she walked away.

As soon as they walked into the apartment, Pierre disappeared down the hall. Noelle knew she should apologize to him, but all she could think about were those boys. She needed advice, and she knew just who to ask.

"Hey," Micah said as soon as her face appeared on the phone screen. When she saw Noelle, she immediately looked concerned. "You okay?"

Noelle felt tears prick the backs of her eyes. She worried if she spoke, she'd cry.

"Is it Tobyn?" Micah asked. That question

made the threat of tears disappear. Noelle felt nervous for a second, worried she was much more transparent than she thought. She frowned, and felt a tickle in her throat, like maybe all her feelings were related to Tobyn, at least a little.

"No. Why would I be upset about Tobyn?"

"I don't know," Micah said. "You guys were being so weird on the roof that I thought maybe you had a fight or something."

"I don't care about Tobyn," Noelle said. She swallowed hard and ignored the fact that it wasn't even close to the truth.

"Okay, okay," Micah said. She rolled her eyes. "My bad. What's wrong then? Something's clearly wrong."

"It's Pierre."

Noelle told her friend about everything that had happened. Micah understood because, ever since her brother had died last summer, she sometimes had panic attacks, too.

"So, they're teasing him about something he can't really control, you know? And I can't walk him home every day," Noelle said. "I don't know what to do."

"That's so messed up," Micah said. "You gotta tell him they're not worth it. That he should ignore them."

Noelle nodded, but deep inside she knew the Lee temper wouldn't allow her brother to do that.

"And if that doesn't work," Micah continued, "because, let's face it, jerky kids like that are hard to ignore, maybe I can ask Ty to swing by and um . . . give them a reason to keep their distance?"

Noelle laughed. "I don't hate that idea," she said. "Tobyn actually scared them off today.

But it just doesn't seem like a real solution."

"Well," Micah said. "Let a girl know. And a girl will get her very cute, very huge boyfriend to take matters into his own hands."

Pierre was playing video games when she got off the phone with Micah. "Hey," she said. He paused his game.

"What?"

"Sorry about earlier."

"I don't know why you were mad at me. I didn't even do anything."

"I know. I wasn't really mad at you."

"Why were you mad then?" he asked. And Noelle shrugged.

"Wanna play?"

He handed her a controller, and she pushed a curl away from where it had fallen in front of her glasses as she took it from him, grateful he always forgave her so quickly and easily.

As they started racing, Pierre started talking trash.

"I'm SO gonna win," he said, grinning.

"Yeah, yeah, yeah. You always do."

Noelle slipped the key into the door at her grandparents' restaurant a few hours before she needed to that Saturday morning. She needed time to think, about Pierre, Tobyn, and everything else, and she thought best on her own.

The glass door of Lee's Dumplings was papered over with menus and flyers, so she couldn't see inside. But the door pushed open easily before she even turned the lock, so she knew someone else was already there.

"Hello?" Noelle said. It had to be her

grandmother, who'd always been an early riser. She could imagine her in the kitchen already tucking thin dumpling skins between her fingers, stuffing them with meaty filling. "Năinai?" She couldn't imagine her grandpa being up this early, but she called out for him, too. "Yéye?"

"In here, Noelle!" her grandmother called.

Noelle only felt a little disappointed she wouldn't be alone when she saw her grandma standing there. Năinai was thin and sturdy, only a few inches shorter than her granddaughter, and she walked as quickly as her fingers folded closed the dumplings in her hands. She smiled at Noelle when she stepped into the kitchen, but didn't stop working. Noelle kissed her on the forehead, and she thought her grandmother's straight black bangs tasted sweet.

Noelle loved the early morning hours when

it was just the two of them prepping food for the day because she often felt out of place when the restaurant was filled with customers. Noelle could tell by the looks on some of their faces that they were surprised to see her, a Black girl, working at a Chinese restaurant. Her parents had always told her she was equally Chinese and Black, but she knew the world didn't see her that way. Luckily her grandparents did, and were quick to correct anyone who dared to say otherwise.

"Come," her grandmother said. "Wash your hands and help."

Noelle bent over the sink and let the hot water rush over her fingers. Her mind spun with thoughts of Tobyn, her brother, and her piece for the showcase. She went to stand beside her grandmother and picked up a small piece of dough, rolled it flat, then reached into the bowl on the counter between them that was full of soft, raw meat that would serve as the dumplings' filling.

They worked silently for only a minute or two before her grandmother said, "Your father told me about your showcase. Me or Yéye will come. We want to hear you play."

She said it simply and she didn't even lift her brown eyes to look up at Noelle as she spoke. "Wait, really?" Noelle asked, because it seemed kind of unbelievable. The only people she knew who worked more than her parents were Năinai and Yéye.

"Yes," her grandmother said, and then in the same breath, "Pay attention, Noelle. You know you need eighteen folds. For luck." She then lifted the dumpling Noelle was closing from her fingers and fixed it before handing it back.

"Why are you here so early?" her

grandmother asked, like she'd just realized what time it was.

"I couldn't sleep," Noelle said, and then, "Pierre's still fighting."

"That boy," her grandmother said, shaking her head. "He should come here and work. That would keep him out of trouble."

It actually wasn't a bad idea. "Yeah," Noelle said. "Yeah, he should!"

"Your father won't want him to," Năinai replied immediately. She shook her head again.

Noelle remembered how upset her father had been when she started working at Lee's the year before. "Why do you think I'm busting my butt downtown?" he said to Yéye. "I don't want my kids to work here."

"A job never hurt anyone," Yéye said. "And it will teach her responsibility, the importance of hard work. When we came here from China—"

"Tell the truth, Bàba. I know why you want them working here."

"Everyone needs to know how to work, Nicholas."

And on it had gone like that. Her father didn't give up until Noelle's mother said, "She wants to, Nick. We can let her keep the money she makes. Does that make it better?"

Her father looked at her then, and Noelle pleaded with him with her eyes. He sighed.

To Noelle, her mother said, "As long as it doesn't interfere with school." Noelle nodded. After that, her father finally agreed.

"But maybe he'd feel differently," Noelle said to her grandmother now, "if it would keep Pierre out of trouble. All his fights happen after school, on the walk home. If he came straight here, maybe . . ."

"I don't know, Noelle. You know how proud

your father can be." Her brother was proud in the same way her father was, so Noelle knew she'd have to do every bit of this perfectly. But she thought it was worth a try.

Noelle pulled out her phone right then and texted her brother.

Hey Big Head. Me and Năinai need your help at Lee's. Mostly your excellent people skills. You know I hate people.

Haha, came his text back. *That's true. What do you want me to do?*

What would you think about coming by on Mondays, Wednesdays, and Fridays to take phone orders? That's when we're busiest, and having you on the phone would be so helpful.

Sure. Sounds easy enough. Plus, free food! But . . .

I know. We gotta ask Dad.

6

Even though it was Saturday, Noelle knew her dad would be working. Her mom worked most weekends, too, but they both always kept their phones on and close by. A few hours later, Noelle dialed her mom's number as soon as they had a lull in the lunch rush at Lee's. It went to voicemail.

After leaving a message, Noelle went back to the kitchen feeling good about her plan. Since Pierre liked the idea, there was no reason she could think of that her mother wouldn't be okay with it, too. If it was three to one, maybe, just maybe, her dad would listen.

"So now you want *both* my kids to work here?" Noelle's father said. He stormed into the kitchen of Lee's Dumplings right before closing, still in his dusty construction clothes. Yéye crossed his arms and turned to face his son. Năinai sighed and murmured something in Mandarin that Noelle didn't understand.

"Oh no," Noelle muttered. She hadn't expected him to find out so soon. This was not a part of her plan and she wondered who had spilled the beans.

Her dad was taller, his shoulders were broader, and his arms were more muscled from building for so many years, but Noelle could see Yéye's features all over her dad's face, especially when he got angry. They had the same narrow eyes and tawny coloring; the same black, messy hair. Noelle often looked for her father's features on her own face, but because she'd inherited her mother's dark skin and thick curls, they were a little harder to find beyond her pin-straight eyelashes. More often, though, she found traces of her father and grandfather in her stubborn pride, and in her own quick, hot temper.

"How did you find out?" she asked him. He spun to face her instead of his parents. "Noelle," he said. "Go home."

"Daddy, just listen for a second," she said. She started to feel angry, too. "Why are you so quick to argue about this? Do you even know why we want him to work here? Have you even heard the reason?"

"I know my parents," her father said.

"Daddy," Noelle said. "Listen. It was my idea. Not theirs. You know how Pierre's been getting into all those fights? I think this could help. I walked home with him the other day and . . . It could at least get him away from those boys a few days a week."

Nick Lee looked at his daughter and clenched his teeth. "Noelle. Let me handle this."

"But did you even ask Pierre how he felt? Or what he thought? Those guys *follow him home*. I can't walk back with him every day because I'd have to leave school early to make it in time. Plus, most days I need to practice cello or come here."

He finally looked like he was listening. His face softened the tiniest bit. "Wait. They follow him?"

Noelle nodded. "I didn't know that either until the other day. You know P is like you.

He wouldn't have told us. He wouldn't have told anyone that they were torturing him."

Noelle's father looked at his parents. He rubbed his temples. "Jesus," he said.

"You don't have to answer now." This came from Năinai. "But just think about it. It could be good for him, son."

Yéye still had his arms crossed.

Early the next morning, Noelle woke up to her parents fighting.

At first, she thought it was about Pierre working, but as she rubbed her eyes and sat up in bed, she listened more closely.

"Fired?" Noelle heard her mother's voice echo down the hall.

"Anaïs, don't worry, I'll find another job."

"Who knows how long that could take, Nick! We can't afford to wait."

Her brother looked at her from his bed on the other side of their room. Noelle got up and poked her head into the hallway. She could feel Pierre behind her listening, too.

"I know. Don't you think I know that? I've already made some calls."

"I knew your temper would get you in trouble down there. Just call your parents," Noelle heard her mother say. "Call your parents and tell them what's happened. They'll let you work at the restaurant until you find something more permanent. The tips alone will be better than nothing."

"No." Noelle saw her father shake his head, hard. "Hell no."

"This is bigger than your ego, Nick. Call them." Her mother handed her father the phone and he looked at her with fire in his eyes.

"Never," he said. Then he walked into the kitchen, grabbed his keys, and left.

Noelle called Năinai. She knew her father would never work there. And she knew there was something else between her father and his parents—something unsaid. But she also knew her family wouldn't be okay with just her mother's salary. What was worse, Noelle thought, was if they needed more of Mama's money here, that would mean less for Granna Esther in Martinique. It was early in hurricane season, and Granna already had a leaking roof.

"Năinai," Noelle said when her grandmother answered. "Can I pick up a few more hours at the restaurant? Maybe work Thursdays and Sundays, too?"

"What about your cello?" Năinai asked. "If you pick up those days that would mean you're here four days in a row. Don't you need time to practice?"

Noelle knew she couldn't tell her the real reason for the extra hours. She could practice at night, or she'd wake up and go to school extra early. She'd spend more time in the music room and less time on Micah's roof with the girls.

"I'll still have time," Noelle assured her. "Don't worry."

"Okay. Well, make sure your dad is okay with it. We don't want another . . . situation."

Noelle lied again. It unnerved her a little, how good she was at it.

"It's money I want to save for college, Nāinai," she told her grandmother in a steady, clear voice. "He'll be okay with me working for that."

"Dad's gonna be pissed if he finds out about this," Pierre said as she hung up.

"Well he better not find out from you," Noelle threatened.

Noelle was in a terrible mood the rest of the day, so she spent most of her time alone. She deep conditioned her hair, stayed in her room playing her cello, and avoided her parents and everyone else. When she got a text from Lux, she started to ignore it, but when she glanced down at it, she saw that it said *I got the goods*.

"What goods?" Noelle asked as soon as Lux answered the phone.

"Well good afternoon to you, too," Lux said. Noelle could see Penny, Lux's stepmother, in the background giving her baby sister a bottle. "Hold on a sec. Let me go somewhere a little more . . . private."

Noelle watched as Lux walked through a few rooms in her father's apartment. It looked much bigger and nicer than the two-bedroom where Noelle and her family lived. Noelle tried not to think about how much better Lux had it, with her big bright bedroom all to herself, but sometimes she couldn't help being a little bit jealous.

Lux stepped into her room and closed the door. "I got the spray paint!" she whispered, her voice full of excitement.

"Oh!" Noelle said. She turned the volume down on her phone. Pierre was playing video games with headphones on, but she didn't want to risk him hearing. "Oh my God," she whispered back. "How?"

"My big cousin," Lux said simply. "He owed me because I watched his big head kid for him yesterday. Ray is a little monster, and my cousin knows it. I told him instead of paying me to just buy me some spray paint."

Noelle laughed. "And he actually did it?"

Lux walked over to her closet and pushed all her sweaters and dresses aside. In the back, behind all of her clothes, was a black trash bag. She pulled it open and there sat a half dozen cans of different colored spray paint.

"Amazing," Noelle said. "I needed some good news today, and this is the best."

"What can I say?" Lux said, shrugging and grinning. "You'd be lost without me."

In orchestra class the next day, Travis sat in the seat right next to first chair, waiting for Noelle when she arrived.

"Ugh," Noelle said. "Can't you take a hint?" But Travis didn't move. "This is the last time I'm going to ask you for the truth," he said.

The truth was Noelle had been up all night practicing so she wouldn't miss a note in orchestra today. The truth was she was freaking out about her father losing his job. She was tired and stressed out and she didn't even know what the truth about herself was yet because she tried her hardest not to think too much about it.

Was she gay, like Tobyn? Or bi? Or even something else? Did this mean she had been lying to Travis when she told him she loved him? Could it be possible for all these things to be true at once?

Instead of saying anything to Travis, she raised her hand and waited for Ms. Porter to call on her. "Travis is bothering me," Noelle said calmly. And Travis said, "Oh my God, no I'm not."

Noelle said, "Yes you are," but she was starting to get mad.

"Travis, please go back to your regular seat."

"I just asked you a question," he said to Noelle, ignoring Ms. Porter. "Why can't you answer a simple question?"

"Because I don't want to! Damn! Leave me alone!"

"Noelle!" Ms. Porter said. "You know that language is unacceptable. As is being this disruptive in class. Travis, get to your seat. And Noelle, I'm giving you detention. Consider this strike two."

After detention, Noelle went to the music room to practice her piece for the showcase. She was so angry about everything that she needed to play to calm herself down. While she'd been in detention, she decided to call her nocturne "Golden Hour," after the Flyy Girls' favorite time to hang out on Micah's rooftop.

She played a few faster pieces until she felt the anger seeping from her bones. Then she fixed her messy curls, straightened her glasses, and pulled out the notes she'd made to the music for "Golden Hour." She'd only practiced that song a few times when the love song she'd begun composing the night of her fight with Tobyn started to fill her head again.

She stopped playing "Golden Hour," looked around at the empty room, and then began to play the ballad. She played slowly at first, letting the music reveal itself, then more quickly as the melody became clearer. She jotted down the notes on the back of the sheet where she'd written the music for the other song, and played it again. *For You*, she thought. The title of this song was "For You," and the "*you*," she knew, could only be Tobyn. The truth of it made her heart feel strange and tight.

She swallowed hard and kept composing. There were high notes that spilled into lower ones. There were moments where the song felt like conversations they'd had, fights, jokes, and everything in between. Noelle kept stopping to write and replay bits and pieces until, two hours later, the whole song was just about done. She wrote the title at the top of her sheet of scribbled music, folded the paper, and tucked it into the side pocket of her backpack.

A week later, Noelle got a new letter from Granna Esther. Her grandmother had written that the rains weren't letting up, that her aunt liked the soup but was still sick, that Noelle should tell Tobyn how she felt. *You're only young once, Little One. Love is rare and only comes but so many times in a young life.* But everything with Tobyn felt farther away and less important than ever. Noelle wrote back right away.

October 26

Bonjou Granna,

I hope you're well. Is your roof
still leaking? I hope you were able
to get it fixed since more hurricanes
are coming. Or, can you stay with
Tantie? Please call when you can. I
tried texting and calling you a few
times but I never heard back. Are my
messages going through?

Daddy got fired. I know he's looking
for another job but I don't know how
long it will take him to find one. Mama
wants him to work at Lee's, but you
know how Daddy is. He refuses even
though I know Nǎinai and Yéye would
let him.

One good thing though is that Pierre is helping out at the restaurant. He hasn't gotten into a fight since he started last week, so it must be helping. Either that or those boys decided to lay off him on their own. Either way, I'm grateful.

Things are still weird with me and Tobyn. I don't think I can tell her how I really feel, at least not yet. But I wrote her a song this afternoon. It was an accident, kind of. Even though I compose sometimes, it's usually way harder, takes way longer. But this one just came out of me. Maybe I'll play it for her. Maybe that could be an easy way to let her know the truth without having to say the words.

Noelle picked up the extra hours at the restaurant, studied when she could, and practiced "For You" in every other free moment she had. With only a little more than two weeks until the fall showcase, she was running out of time to perfect her piece. She'd completely ditched her original idea of performing "Golden Hour" at the showcase because the song she'd written for Tobyn wouldn't leave her mind.

Noelle felt tired, exhausted really, and barely sleeping was taking its toll. She felt more of her meanness slipping out in big and small ways with her parents, her friends, even with teachers at school.

Noelle argued with her mom and dad when she overslept the second Monday morning after working all weekend at the restaurant. "You think I want to be late on purpose?" she said, and her mother shot back, "I don't know who you think you're talking to, young lady," at the same time as her dad said, "Watch your mouth."

She said, "Ugh," threw on her glasses, and left the house in a rush.

Later that day, while they were eating in the Yard, Tobyn asked about Travis. "I haven't seen him hanging around in a while. Did you guys have a fight or something?"

"We didn't have a fight."

"Where's he been then?"

"Yeah," Micah said. "I'd noticed, too. Why

aren't you guys hanging out?"

"Oh my God, can you guys get off my back? We broke up. Not that it's any of your business."

"Oh," Tobyn said. "Our bad. But chill, Noelle. We didn't know."

When Micah asked if Noelle was okay, and Lux asked why they'd ended things, Noelle packed up her stuff and left the lunch table without answering.

On Tuesday, she flipped out on Micah when she said she was worried her piece wouldn't be ready in time for the showcase. "If you spent half the time you spend complaining actually painting, maybe you'd be done already."

That afternoon, she got into it with Lux when she told Noelle she wasn't sure if she could hide the spray paint anymore. "My dad's been snooping around. And there's no way I could hide it at my mom's."

"Do I have to do everything?" Noelle spat. "If you can't figure out how to hide it, just bring it to school tomorrow and I'll figure it out myself."

But unlike her family and her other friends, Lux was not the one. "You don't just get to say whatever you want, you know. You better be careful or you'll end up with no friends at all."

Noelle knew Lux was right, and by Wednesday, she had calmed down enough to apologize for it all. She brought the girls their favorite treats from the restaurant, did a few extra chores for her parents, took Pierre for ice cream, and worked hard to get her temper in check so she wouldn't do any of it again. But there was always a point during every day when the broken pieces of herself that she'd carefully put back together shattered all over again.

It happened whenever Noelle heard her

mother ask her dad, "Any luck?" and her father answered sharply, "Don't you think I'd tell you if anything had changed, Anaïs? You can stop asking."

She turned down the girls when they asked her to hang out over the weekend and most of the next week because she needed the time to work and practice. Besides, she was convinced that if she didn't get it together, her unpredictable anger would ruin whatever was left of her relationships.

On Thursday, the day before the showcase, Noelle headed to school early to use the music room before anyone else got there.

She felt tired as usual—she'd convinced her grandmother to let her work the night before and stayed at the restaurant until closing. Instead of setting her music stand to face the door, she faced the windows at the back of the music room while she played. She didn't want to have to make small talk with anyone who peeked or came inside.

She heard the door to the music room open just when she began to play "For You" one last time before class started. She played like she was alone, even though she knew she wasn't. As she played she forgot all her worries and only thought of Tobyn.

The song was slow and soft at the beginning, the way her feelings for Tobyn had started. Noelle had been watching her friend talk one day when Tobyn let out a sudden, wild laugh. Noelle heard something inside her, like a tiny whisper. *She's pretty when she laughs like that.* And then, *She's always pretty.*

The song quickened in the middle, the notes jumping up and down the way Noelle's heart started to a few months ago whenever Tobyn was close by. Before, she wouldn't hesitate to push Tobyn playfully or braid her friend's hair, but now . . . the thought of touching Tobyn made Noelle feel like she might pass out.

The song changed again right before the end. This part sounded angry and represented all the dark parts of their friendship. The fights they had. The way Noelle felt when Tobyn talked about Ava. All the mean things she'd ever done or said. Noelle always played this part of the song with a frown wrinkling the center of her forehead.

As she got closer to the end, the melody slowed down again. Here was where Noelle played out how she was dying to kiss Tobyn, to tell her about how she made her feel. She remembered Tobyn handing her the doughnut and the way their hands had touched, and that streak of blue in Tobyn's hair.

She finished the song, and someone behind her started clapping. When Noelle turned around, she saw Tobyn standing there looking beautiful.

"Hey Noelle," Tobyn said. "Sorry to interrupt. It's just . . . things have been weird with us for a while and it feels like I haven't seen you. I know you're really busy, but I wanted to make sure you were okay."

Noelle laid her cello in its case. Maybe what happened next was because the song was still fresh in her mind, in her heart, in her very fingers. Or it happened because Tobyn had said her name. Noelle was still holding her bow when she stepped closer to her friend, closer than she'd allowed herself in weeks. Quick as the middle section of the love song she'd just played, Noelle leaned forward and kissed her.

Tobyn pulled back.

"Noelle," she said. She looked confused, and nervous, *and something else*, Noelle thought. "You know I have a girlfriend."

Of course Noelle knew that. She didn't know what had made her do something so stupid. She felt the hot flush of embarrassment pass over her face and spread down her neck, and she was grateful for her dark skin, her long hair—they allowed her to hide. She let her curls fall over her glasses so Tobyn wouldn't see her eyes as they filled, instantly, with tears.

"Ava doesn't even love you anymore!" Noelle shouted. "You said it yourself." Noelle felt that familiar meanness swelling inside her. "But maybe you're just too clueless and desperate to believe it."

"Why would you say that?" Tobyn asked quietly. "I told you that in confidence."

Noelle didn't know why. But she ran from the room, leaving her cello right there on the music room floor.

Noelle went straight home, closed her bedroom door and cried, curled in a tight ball in the center of her bed. But minutes after she'd arrived, her father walked into the apartment.

Noelle tried to be quiet, but a soft sob slipped out and it echoed loud enough for her father to hear. Noelle heard his footsteps as he approached her room. He eased open her door.

"Noelle? What are you doing here? Why aren't you at school?" he asked her. She rolled over to face him, and when he saw her tears, he came closer. "Noelle, honey. What's wrong?"

"It's too much," Noelle said.

"What is?"

"Everything."

Her father's face turned stormy. "I knew I shouldn't have let you work," he said.

"No, Daddy. It's not that!" But it was and it wasn't.

"It's the showcase. And I mean, yeah, I'm worried about family stuff and Mama, too. You know how stressed she is."

Her father nodded. "But honey. It's my job to worry about this family, not yours."

"But what about Granna Esther? Whose job is it to worry about her?"

"Ours. Your mother's and mine."

Noelle shook her head. "I can't just not worry about this stuff, though. I want to help. Why won't you just work with Nǎinai and Yéye?"

Her father swallowed. "We have a long history. Me and your grandparents. Stuff I don't really like talking about. But I can't work for them ever again. Just believe me when I say it's more than pride," he said. But Noelle wasn't sure that was true.

"Are you ready for the showcase?" he asked. "Since I'm funemployed," he joked, "I'll be there."

Noelle looked up at him. "Really? You're coming?"

He nodded. She wrapped her arms around him and felt something heavy lift from her shoulders.

"I have an interview," he said. "Things will be better soon. I promise. And in the meantime, I need you to trust me to take care of you."

He looked at her and used his thumbs to wipe away her tears.

"Okay. Thank you," she said.

9

Friday the thirteenth of November was the night of the showcase, and Noelle was nervous. Not about performing. She'd practiced "For You" so many times that she could play the song in her sleep. Noelle was nervous about seeing Tobyn. She was nervous because her family would be in the audience watching her for the first time in her recent memory.

The visual artists set up their work in the hallway outside the auditorium, so the first hour of the showcase was dedicated to letting everyone roam around and look at sketches, paintings, sculptures, and photography. Noelle went by and saw Micah's painting. It was a huge portrait of her brother, Milo. "Oh, Micah," Noelle said. "I see why you were worried about finishing it now. But it looks so good, girl."

Micah grinned.

Lux's piece featured a series of photographs of different parts of her body that she mosaicked together to make a fractured self-portrait. Noelle loved it, and so did the gathered crowd. Noelle gave Lux a thumbs-up from where she stood.

When it was almost time for the second part of the showcase to start, Noelle joined the rest of the performance arts students backstage. She made sure her cello was tuned and swiped her bow hair with rosin.

She saw Tobyn sipping from a thermos across the busy room. Noelle knew it was full of warm water with honey and lemon, Tobyn's favorite before-singing drink. And then, a moment later, Tobyn turned and saw her. There were dozens of people between them playing instruments and talking—a few were even dancing—but something about the way Tobyn looked at Noelle made her feel like they were alone. She took a few deep breaths when Tobyn didn't immediately turn away from her.

Noelle started toward her friend, but when she was only a few steps away, Ava appeared out of nowhere and wrapped her arms around Tobyn's waist. Tobyn only hesitated for a second before she hugged her girlfriend back. "Good luck, bae," Noelle heard Ava say. Tobyn watched Noelle over Ava's shoulder. "You too, boo," Tobyn said.

Noelle turned and quickly went back to the corner where she'd left her cello. She needed to focus on what she was about to do, not the girl hugging someone else half a room away.

Noelle listened to Tobyn sing right by the edge of the curtain. The song sounded bright and clear, and Noelle couldn't help but imagine Tobyn accompanying her as she played "For You." She didn't know what the words to her song would be, just that Tobyn was the only person who could sing them.

Noelle left the edge of the stage just before the audience began to applaud Tobyn's performance. She pulled out her phone and sent her friend a text.

I can't even tell you how sorry I am for what I said, T. But this song I'm about to play . . . I wrote it for you. Wait for me in the second-floor bathroom if you think you can forgive me. I'll explain everything.

Noelle felt like she was hiding as she played, but also like she was finally revealing all of her best-kept secrets. She had sheets of music on a stand in front of her, but she kept her eyes shut for the entire performance and only opened them as she played the final note.

The audience exploded in applause and Noelle couldn't hide her grin as she stood and bowed.

Once she got back behind the curtain, and as soon as she could get away from all her teachers gushing about her piece, she raced to the second floor of Augusta Savage, looking for Tobyn. And she was there waiting as soon as Noelle pushed open the bathroom door, leaning against one of the shiny white sinks.

"You wrote that," Tobyn said, "for me?" Noelle let the door close behind her. She nodded slowly. "And you kissed me." That part wasn't a question, but Noelle nodded again anyway. "And then said that really mean thing to me." Noelle looked away.

"Why?" Tobyn asked.

"So many reasons," Noelle said, and she felt sweat trickling down her back and beading across her forehead. "I . . . care about you, Tobyn."

"Of course you do," Tobyn said. "I care about you, too. You're one of my best friends."

Noelle shook her head. "I care about you more . . . no, *differently* . . . than how I care about Micah and Lux and everyone else."

Noelle stepped closer to Tobyn, who was staring at her like she still didn't understand.

"But you were with Travis," Tobyn said. "You've always only been with boys."

"Yeah. I know it's confusing," Noelle agreed. "I'm confused, too. Not about how I feel about you. More about what it means, I guess. How to handle it. What I should do next."

Tobyn turned and looked in the mirror that ran the length of the wall over the sinks. She looked at Noelle through the glass instead of directly and said, "Oh."

"And I wanted to apologize. For what I said about Ava. It's no excuse, but I was feeling so . . . I don't know. Scared I guess. Rejected. I should never have said that. And I don't know how Ava feels about you. But if she doesn't love you anymore, she's the biggest idiot on earth."

Tobyn bit her lip.

"I . . . know this is a lot," Noelle admitted. "And I get it if you feel like this is coming out of nowhere. But I don't think I can hide how I feel anymore."

Tobyn still didn't say anything. Noelle felt sick.

"I won't try to kiss you again. I shouldn't have done that in the first place. But Tobyn— and I hope you don't hate me for saying this; I hope it doesn't ruin everything—I do *want* to kiss you again. I've wanted to kiss you for months."

Noelle found Tobyn's eyes in the mirror, and then Tobyn turned and looked at her dead on. "But, like, I don't know what to *do* with that, Noelle. Sometimes you act like you don't even like me. You're always so mean."

Noelle bit her bottom lip. "I know," she said. She was worried she'd said sorry too much, though, and that she hadn't *done* enough to show how much she meant it, so she didn't say it again.

"So, you *do* like me?" Tobyn asked.

"I more than like you, Tobyn," Noelle replied.

"Do Micah and Lux know?" Tobyn asked.

"No."

"Does anyone?"

"No. Unless you count my grandmother in Martinique."

Tobyn frowned so Noelle explained. "I wrote to her about you."

Tobyn pushed away from the sinks and crossed her arms. "I need some time to think," she said. "And you know I'm still with Ava."

"I know." But secretly Noelle hoped she wouldn't be for long. She'd told her to dump her in anger, but she'd meant it. Tobyn deserved better. "I just needed to tell you."

Tobyn nodded, then she grinned a little. "I mean, I get it. I *am* pretty cute." She pretended to brush dust off her shoulder, and fluff her fro. Noelle laughed a little, full of relief.

"One more thing though," Tobyn said. Noelle turned to face her friend, and Tobyn's dark eyes were bright and fierce.

"I won't be anyone's secret," she said.

Noelle and Tobyn went back down to the auditorium. Once all the performances were over, they found their families in the crowded hall. Noelle ran over to her father and brother as soon as she spotted them, and Pierre handed her a blooming bouquet of wildflowers. "I still can't believe you came," Noelle said to her dad.

"You were outstanding, Noelle. I know we hear you play all the time at home, but I'm sad it's been so long since I've seen you on stage."

Yéye nodded, agreeing. "We will try to come more often," he said. "You go to college so soon."

Năinai just smiled and patted Noelle's hand, and she knew that was her grandmother's way of saying she was proud.

"Excuse me?"

A voice that Noelle didn't recognize came from somewhere behind her. When Noelle turned her head toward the sound, a tall East Asian woman was smiling at her.

"Hi, Noelle. My name is Penelope Chung. I'm a scout for the Manhattan School of Music."

Noelle turned around fully to face her, heart thumping. "Oh. Hi," she said.

Penelope smiled. "I loved your piece. I was wondering if you've decided on a conservatory or where you'd like to study next year?"

After Noelle and her father had spoken to

Penelope for a while, and Noelle had taken the scout's thick, creamy business card and tucked it into the pocket of her cello case, she left her family to look for her friends. But she bumped into Travis instead.

"Hi," she said.

"Hey," he said.

"Look. I wasn't ready to tell you this before, but I think I am now. I broke up with you because I liked someone else."

"Why couldn't you just tell me that?" Travis asked.

"Because. It's a girl. And it's . . . complicated."

"Oh," Travis said. He looked a little confused, but Noelle pushed forward.

"I loved you, though," Noelle promised. "My feelings were real."

"I loved you, too. So thanks for telling me the truth."

10

Noelle's father had told her not to worry, so over the next couple of weeks she tried her hardest not to. She'd gotten back on Ms. Porter's good side by playing perfectly for weeks in a row and cut back her hours at Lee's. She was grateful to have the time back, but she still saved her tips . . . just in case. The showcase was behind her, but after meeting the scout and speaking to her about the real possibility of attending, Noelle wanted to hold on to first chair and go to the Manhattan School of Music even more than she had before.

"Let me see that card," Micah said.

Noelle had invited her friends over to her place to apologize to them again. She'd brought a bunch of dumplings home from the restaurant. Lux sat on Noelle's bedroom floor, feet propped against the edge of the dresser. Micah sat in Noelle's desk chair backward, and Tobyn lay on her stomach on Noelle's bed, her chin propped on one hand when she wasn't taking bites out of the bao she held in the other.

Noelle handed over Penelope Chung's card. "Email me when you submit your application," Penelope had told her. "I'll do what I can to fast-track it through admissions."

"Whoa," Micah said, reading it. "She sounds like a big shot."

"I know," Noelle agreed. "She told me to apply and send in a video for the pre-screening.

Then I'll find out after a few weeks if I'm picked to audition in person."

"They have a bunch of programs," Lux said. She pulled up the school's website on her phone. "There's Classical, Orchestral, Contemporary . . . You can play all that stuff. What are you gonna apply for? You have to pick, right?"

Noelle nodded. "Yeah. I'm not sure yet."

"Can I see that?" Tobyn asked. She reached over the edge of the bed and snatched up Lux's phone. "What about Composition? You write songs all the time."

Noelle looked at the card so she didn't have to look at anyone else. She wondered if Tobyn was waiting for her to say something about "For You"; to tell the girls that she'd written it for Tobyn.

When Noelle glanced back up she said,

"I don't know if I've written enough to be a composition major. I don't think I'd want to *have* to write. I want that to be something I do when I want to, or just for fun."

Micah and Lux nodded. Tobyn looked at the phone and didn't meet Noelle's eyes.

They were all figuring out what they'd be doing after graduation. Micah showed her friends the long list of colleges she was applying to—it was on a spreadsheet complete with scholarships she needed to apply for, application costs, and deadlines. "This level of organization is so on-brand for you, Micah," Tobyn said, laughing. And Micah poked out her tongue.

Lux was thinking about taking a year off before she went to college—if she went at all. "I want to travel," Lux told them. "Take my camera and see everything. I've been looking for ways I can travel for free, like work exchanges and stuff. My dad definitely doesn't want me to take any time off, but my moms is cool with it. I'll be eighteen soon, so I'm gonna do whatever I want."

Tobyn grabbed Noelle's pillow and hugged it. She stared at the ceiling and talked about joining her sister's band. "Devyn said I could sing with them, do gigs and stuff, tour. They've gotten a little better so they're playing more and more. But I really just wanna be famous."

Noelle let them talk. She listened and stayed quiet, thinking about how her pillow was going to smell like Tobyn's hair; wondering if she should have said more about the song. She still wasn't ready to tell Lux and Micah the truth about her feelings.

A little while later, while they were talking about other things, Noelle got an idea. "Micah, since your applications are due around the same time as mine, and since Lux is applying for that work exchange the same week, why don't we do the prank then? It could be symbolic, like, a celebration of officially getting out of here."

Micah let out a little squeal, and Lux said, "Badass," and Tobyn grinned. "Let's do it," they all said. Noelle marked the calendar hanging on her wall with a big red X.

In Granna Esther's next letter, she told Noelle not to worry about her father. *He's the grown-up, you're the child,* she'd written. *It's his job to take care of you, Little One.* She told Noelle that they were weathering the storms well, though the house creaked loudly because of the winds and sometimes it kept her awake at night. *Our Internet has been spotty, so some of your calls and texts weren't getting through. Your aunt is better and your cousins came to visit so I've had a good week. Please tell your mother we're grateful for whatever she can spare. How did your showcase go?*

December 2

Bonjou Granna Esther,

The showcase went really, really well. You'll never believe this, but there was a scout there. She was from the Manhattan School of Music, and after the show she gave me her card. She told me I should apply and I'm definitely going to.

I guess I have a lot of big news.

I also kinda kissed Tobyn? I know, I know. I can't believe I did it, either. But after the kiss we talked and I was honest with her. At least now she knows how I feel.

Travis does, too. I told him the truth that I loved him, but that I like someone else. I haven't told my friends yet, though. Even though it gave Travis some closure, I still have a lot of questions. But I don't have any answers.

Noelle had no idea how to use Lux's fancy camera, which she'd borrowed to record her pre-screening video for her Manhattan School of Music application. Lux showed her a few basic things, but she couldn't imagine playing "For You" with Lux watching.

At the showcase it had been different because she could barely see the audience thanks to the bright stage lights. Playing for an audience of one was much scarier—she worried all the softest, saddest parts of her would show.

"I'm not an idiot," Noelle said to Lux just to get her to leave so she could record it on her own. Then Lux said, "Fine. You know everything apparently. Good luck," and left.

Now Noelle regretted it, but she felt too embarrassed to ask Lux to come back.

Micah was away this weekend and she thought about calling Tobyn, but she wasn't ready to be alone with her again. And when she asked Pierre, he couldn't figure it out, either.

"Those kids still messing with you on the walk home?" Noelle asked. Pierre hadn't come home bloody or crying in weeks. Even with the hours he spent at the restaurant she wondered if they'd laid off him completely.

"Not since Ty," Pierre said, then stopped.

"Not since Ty what?" Noelle asked.

Pierre fiddled with the camera. "He came to school the week after you and Tobyn picked me up. I don't know what he said to them, but they haven't messed with me since."

Noelle laughed to herself. Micah had sent Ty after all.

"Ask Daddy to help you," Pierre told her, handing the camera back. "You know he's good at this kind of stuff."

"I thought he was busy," Noelle said. Pierre laughed. "I'm pretty sure he's playing Tetris."

Noelle went into the living room, and sure enough, it looked like her father was playing a game.

"I thought you had an interview," Noelle said.

"I did. It didn't go well."

Noelle crossed her arms. She pushed down the anger and worry that made its way up her throat. "Does Mom know?"

"No. I didn't even tell her I had the interview. I didn't want to get her hopes up." He finally turned to look at Noelle and said, "I shouldn't have gotten yours up, either."

Noelle sighed and held out the camera. "Well, since you're not doing anything important." She looked at the computer. "Can you help me with this?"

He tried a few times, but he couldn't figure it out, either.

"Just ask your friend to help you," he told her, handing the camera back. "Don't be so proud, kid." Noelle couldn't believe he of all people would say that to her.

"You're such a hypocrite," she said.

"What?" He whirled on her, and she could tell he was pissed. "I don't know where you got that mouth, but it's going to get you in serious trouble one day if you don't watch yourself."

In that moment, Noelle realized that she often said things she immediately wanted to take back because she felt exposed or ashamed. Just like her dad did. Noelle stared at her father, and she knew right then that she didn't want to be the mean girl anymore.

"Okay, Daddy. Sorry. Look. How about we make a deal," she said.

Her father squinted and spoke slowly. "What kind of deal?"

"My deadline for this application is December fifteenth, and I'll probably turn everything in way before then." She squinted up at him. "If you don't have a new job by then, you have to call Nǎinai and Yéye and work at the restaurant until you find something better."

Her father shook his head and said, "Sometimes you're just like your mother." But then he smirked.

"Deal," he said.

They'd all agreed to meet at Lux's apartment after school the following Monday to talk about the final details of the prank, but Tobyn was late. Noelle checked her phone but she didn't have any new messages.

"Oh, she texted me," Micah said. "She can't come. Something about meeting up with Ava." She shrugged.

"She's always with Ava," Noelle said, and to stop herself from rolling her eyes, she took off her glasses and cleaned them with the hem of her shirt. "I thought she was going to break up with her."

Lux laughed. "Why'd you think that? Just because you told her to?"

Yes, Noelle thought, but didn't say. And because of the kiss. She shrugged. "Well she does usually listen to me. All of you do," she added, smiling sweetly.

Micah shook her head. "You think everyone listens to you, Noelle, when really we're just doing whatever we want but not telling you, so we don't have to deal with you saying something annoying."

Lux raised her eyebrows, like she was surprised Micah had the guts to say what she'd just said.

"What?" Noelle asked. She looked back and forth between Lux and Micah. "What does that mean?"

Micah's face looked full of regret. "Nothing,"

she muttered. "Can we just get back to the prank?"

"No," Noelle said. "I want to wait for Tobyn."

"She's not coming, Noelle," Lux said. "I saw her last night and I think she's mad at you about something."

Micah said, "Yep. I talked to her this morning. She definitely is."

Tobyn *had* seemed distant this past week, but Noelle had been trying to ignore it. She'd been telling herself Tobyn was busy. But Lux and Micah were still hanging out with and talking to Tobyn. Tobyn's silence suddenly felt a lot more personal.

"Why would she be mad?" Noelle asked quietly.

Lux shrugged. "I asked her. She wouldn't say."

"It could really be anything, though," Micah said. And Lux agreed. "Yep. You say all kinds of nasty things to all of us, all the time, Noelle. Not gonna lie, it's getting old."

"You think this, too, Micah?" Noelle asked. Micah kind of half-shrugged like she agreed but wished she didn't.

"Like when I told you about hiding the spray paint? Or like when I let you borrow my camera and you were all snippy for no reason?" Lux said.

"Yeah, or like before the showcase when I told you I was worrying about finishing? And I mean, you're the worst with Tobyn. Especially when it has anything to do with Ava," Micah added.

"Yeah, you treat Ava like crap. But what did she ever do to you?" Lux asked.

Micah frowned and nodded at the same time. "Come to think of it, what did *we* ever do to you?"

Noelle felt her mouth go dry. "What is this? An intervention?"

"Nah," Lux said. Her face looked serious. "We'd never do that without T."

Noelle felt hot and embarrassed. And she missed Tobyn. She'd been looking forward to seeing her here tonight because she hadn't really spoken to her since all four of them had hung out in her room. It made the mean thing inside her flare, like a lit matchstick. But this time, she didn't let the ugliness out.

"I think I'm like my dad," Noelle almost whispered.

"Huh?" Lux said, at the same time as Micah asked, "What?"

"I realized it recently. How much I'm like my dad. That I say messed-up stuff to the people I love when I'm scared."

"I still don't get it. Why would you be scared

around us?" Lux asked.

"Because," Noelle answered. "There's stuff about me you don't know."

"Like what?" Micah asked.

"Like my dad lost his job, so I worked extra hours to help out with our bills."

"Whoa, really?" Micah said.

Lux looked at her hands.

"Like, I'm worried about my grandma in Martinique. I'm worried about getting into college. I'm worried about all these new . . . feelings . . . inside me. I'm always worried about everything."

Micah said, "Why didn't you tell us, Noelle?"

Noelle felt her eyes well with tears. "Like, you don't know that I like Tobyn. That's why I broke up with Travis. I kissed her, and that's probably why she's mad at me, even though she said she wasn't."

"Wait . . . You *kissed* Tobyn?" Lux said.

"Holy—" Micah said.

Noelle squeezed her eyes shut tight. Tears rolled down her cheeks. "Don't tell Tobyn I told you. I gotta go."

Noelle and her mom were rarely home at the same time. But that day, when Noelle opened the door to her family's apartment, both her mom and dad were sitting at the kitchen table with Pierre.

"Hey," she said, trying to sound normal. But her voice came out all wrong.

"Noelle?" her mother said. "You okay?"

Noelle started to nod, but a second later, she burst into tears again. Pierre jumped up, ran over, and hugged her. Her mother looked really uncomfortable, and Noelle thought about how she had never seen her mom cry. Her father's eyes went soft around the edges, though, and glanced over at her mom. Without speaking, his expression seemed to say, *I think she needs you more than me right now.*

Noelle hugged her brother back. Then she said, "I'm fine," but it seemed clear to everyone in the kitchen that she wasn't. Noelle's mother put her arm around her shoulder. "Want to talk about it?"

NO, Noelle wanted to say. The word flew to her lips like a reflex, but it wasn't true. She swallowed it whole, looked at her mom, and nodded.

"So, what happened?" Anaïs asked her daughter.

"I'm afraid I'm ruining everything," Noelle said.

"Why do you think that?" her mother asked.

Noelle told her about what had happened at Lux's, and also about how she'd snapped at them all when she was practicing for the showcase while balancing all the extra hours at Lee's. "I apologized," Noelle insisted, "to everyone. But I guess that wasn't good enough."

"I know I'm not here a lot," her mom said. "I know I'm always working. But I also know *you*, Noelle. You can be snippy when you're under a lot of pressure, or when you're upset, or when you feel powerless. The great irony is you're worse to those closest to you. But you don't want to constantly test your friends' love for you. You don't want to push them away."

"Sometimes I do," Noelle said, and her mother laughed. "But I always want them to come back."

Anaïs grinned. "That's the key. If you want

them around, don't give them a reason to leave."

Noelle was about to ask her mother what she should do now, but she heard her father's gruff voice from the hallway.

"Anaïs," he called. They listened to his quick footsteps and he stepped back into the kitchen a second later. There was a thin white envelope in his hand.

He looked between the two of them. "What is this?" he asked.

13

December 10

Bonjou Granna,

Everything's a mess.

My friends think I'm this terrible person, and to be honest, I can't blame them.

Tobyn isn't speaking to me. She's upset, I guess about the kiss, but I don't know for sure because she won't return any of my texts or calls.

Remember that scout I told you about? She emailed me asking if I'd sent in my application yet, and I haven't because I can't figure out the damn camera, and I'm too ashamed to ask Lux for help.

As if all of that wasn't terrible enough, something bad happened tonight. I'd saved all my tips from work, sealed them up in an envelope, and put the envelope in Mama's dresser. She didn't know about it. Neither did Daddy. And he'd even made a deal with me to work at the restaurant if he didn't find a job by December 15th. But then he found the envelope.

He lost it. I tried to explain; I told him I did this behind Mama's back and not to be upset at her. He said he was responsible for this family, not his parents. Then Mama got mad and said, "Well how about you swallow your pride and take responsibility for once?"

It was ugly. Mama went to their bedroom and slammed the door and Daddy stormed out. And I feel like the whole thing, plus everything else that's a mess in my life, is all my fault.

Noelle's father came home a few hours later. She was terrified her parents would break up because of this, because of *her*, so there was no way she could sleep. When her father walked back into the apartment, she ran to the door and hugged him. "I thought you weren't coming back," she said. He kissed the top of her head.

"Of course I was coming back," he replied.

"Don't be mad at Mama. Don't be mad at Nǎinai and Yéye, either. Why does everything related to Lee's make you so mad?"

Her father slipped out of his jacket and hung it on the hook by the door.

"Your Yéye, he got sick when I was eighteen, and if I didn't help out, we could have lost the restaurant," her father said.

"Your Nǎinai, she told me to go to college, but I wouldn't have been able to bear moving away, knowing that my parents were going to lose their business because my mom was taking care of my sick dad. So I stayed. I deferred my admission for a year, but I lost my scholarships. I decided not to take out loans because I was too afraid of the debt, so I just never went back to school. I worked at Lee's for a long time, until the restaurant started to make a good profit. Then I noticed my parents were paying me more than I'd earned. When I asked them to stop, they said they wanted to repay me for staying while Dad was sick. I told them not to do that but they wouldn't listen, so as soon as I could, I found another job."

Noelle had no idea about her father's history with her grandparents. "It would be different," her father continued, "if they just wanted to help out of the goodness of their hearts. What I hate is that they feel indebted to me. After everything they've done for me for my whole life, they don't want to 'owe' me, when I never said that they did."

Noelle looked at her father. "That's why you didn't want me or Pierre to work there?" He nodded. "Because you were afraid they'd use us to repay you?"

"Yeah," he said. "I know we need some help right now, but I don't want it from them."

Noelle could see that pride had been the root of all of this. She didn't want to let her pride poison her relationships the way it seemed to be working its way through her family. She wanted to be more like her Granna, to ask for help when she needed it—to accept generosity when it was offered. She wanted to be kinder and less angry all the time.

I told them, Noelle texted Tobyn. *Micah and Lux know everything.*

What did they say? Tobyn answered. It was the first time she'd answered one of Noelle's texts in a while.

Nothing, Noelle said. *I mean, I left right after I told them.*

And how do you feel? Tobyn asked. *Knowing that they know.*

I don't know, Tobyn. It just felt like I should tell them.

Tobyn went quiet, and while Noelle could see that she'd read her messages, Tobyn didn't send anything else. *Tobyn, don't shut me out. I'm sorry about telling you to break up with Ava. Is that why you're mad?*

Read, but no answer.

You really want things to end like this?

Tobyn didn't text back.

When Noelle's grandmother wrote back, she told her to focus on one problem at a time. *Focus on your friends first,* Granna Esther had written. *Friends are everything in this life. Why not write them a song?* she suggested. *They will forgive you the second they hear your beautiful music.*

Noelle had already written her friends a song, and she remembered it as soon as she read Granna Esther's words. She knew exactly what she needed to do.

Can you guys meet me at Micah's? Noelle sent this text to the group chat. The whole chain had been pretty quiet lately, and Noelle knew the three of her friends were probably texting together on a separate chain without her. She tried not to let it bother her too much.

Sure, Lux sent. *Micah, when's good?*

Whenever, Micah sent next.

But there was one person who hadn't responded.

Tobyn? Noelle sent. *I really want all of us to be there.*

A good twenty minutes passed before Tobyn finally responded.

K. I'll come.

It was mid-December, and the weather had cooled quickly, so Micah had on a puffy jacket and thick pink scarf when she opened the door that lead from the stairwell. "You're the first one here," Micah said.

Micah dragged a few of the lawn chairs to the center of the roof, and Noelle grabbed a stool that she set up a little farther away. "What's this about, Noelle?" Micah asked. "The prank?"

Noelle had almost forgotten all about that.

"No," Noelle answered.

"The kiss?" Micah asked. She smirked, and Noelle shook her head.

"You'll see in a few. I want to wait until everyone is here."

Noelle cupped her hands and blew on them

before reaching down to pop open her cello case. She prepped her bow and made sure her cello was tuned.

Lux poked her head through the door a few minutes later. "Hey," she said. "We finally gonna talk about you *kissing* Tobyn?"

Noelle felt her face heat up. "I like her. I don't really know what else there is to say about it."

"Uh, how about where and when did it happen? Did she know you liked her before it happened? Is that why she's being all weird around us now?" Lux said.

"Are you two in loooooove?" Micah added.

"It happened at school in the music room. I've liked her for a while. I don't know if that's why she's being weird."

"That's not why," Tobyn said as she stepped through the door. "I just needed some space and time to think."

They all went quiet as Tobyn walked toward Noelle. Micah and Lux watched, and Noelle didn't know what Tobyn was about to do or say. She was too nervous to wait to find out.

She lifted her bow and started playing. Tobyn stopped in her tracks.

The song sounded bright at the beginning. It shined, like the sun glinting off the windows of the buildings they could see from the roof. And as she continued to play, the high notes fell deeper and seemed to come from the belly of the instrument. It then faded a bit and got softer. The song felt a little sad near the end, the way the end of most days could feel, like something about it had been shattered. But even with the parts that sounded broken, the song still felt like the four of them—pieces of a whole.

When she finished playing, the girls applauded. "That was another original, wasn't it?" Tobyn asked. And Noelle nodded.

"It's called 'Golden Hour.' I wrote it about us. I know a song doesn't fix everything, or anything really," Noelle said, "but I want you to take this song as a promise."

"A promise?" Micah asked.

"A promise that from this point forward I'm going to change the way I talk to you guys. I can't say I'll never be a smartass ever again, but I will say I won't speak when I'm angry or irritated or stressed out. I'm learning that meanness can fester," Noelle said. "And I don't want to become this person who is horrible to the people I love."

"That makes sense," Micah said.

"But how can we believe you?" Lux asked.

"You just gotta trust," Tobyn said. "I think she can do it."

They had planned to pull off their prank the same day that Noelle submitted her application to the Manhattan School of Music. She'd already uploaded the video Lux had helped her record, copied and pasted the essay Micah had read over for her, and attached the artistic resume that Tobyn helped her pull together at the last minute (she'd had no idea she needed one). Now she typed in the numbers of Năinai's credit card for the application fee. "You can take it out of my tips," Noelle told her grandmother when she'd asked to borrow her card. "No, honey," Nǎinai replied. "We're happy to pay for this. We're proud of you."

Noelle hit send on the application with her fingers and toes crossed. Then shot a quick email to Penelope Chung to let her know her application was complete.

She grabbed her heavy cello case and backpack and was ready to slip out of the room before Pierre woke up, but when she checked her phone, she saw that she had a string of texts from her friends.

Lux: *Soooo my dad found the spray paint when he went into my closet looking for his snow boots this morning . . .*

Tobyn: *crap crap crap*

Micah: *Oh no Lux! Are you okay?*

Tobyn: *Did he call you Luxana and take your whole life away?*

Lux: *Lol. Yeah, I'm fine. I lied and said it was*

for a photography project, but he's still pissed that I got it in a shady way and he won't let me have the paint back. Soooo . . . do we have a backup plan?

Micah: *Maybe we just wait? Do it later in the year or something?*

Tobyn: *Noelle, where are you????*

Lux: *That girl better not have overslept if I'M up!*

Noelle looked out her window and saw that it must have snowed heavily while they slept.

"Dammit," Noelle whispered. Their plans were ruined, but she immediately tried to come up with a new idea.

It was so early that the streetlights were still on and the only cars on the road were the snow trucks plowing and salting the streets. Snow was still falling. As she watched the trucks shove snow into huge piles against the curbs, she got an idea for how their prank might not be ruined, not exactly. She picked up her phone to text her friends back.

Don't worry, Noelle sent. *I have an idea.*

Meet me in front of school like we planned.

Bring shovels.

And Kool-Aid.

Lux was the only one who replied:

Kool-Aid?????

The other Flyy Girls were already in front of the school when Noelle arrived a half hour later. It was still very early, and the sun barely peeked through the tall buildings all around them.

"It's like another Golden Hour," Micah said.

Lux groaned. "Yeah, one I'd be fine with

never seeing again. Why did we have to do this so early?" she whined.

"Because doing it at night would be too risky," Tobyn reminded her. "Duh." She yawned. "Let's just get started. We don't have much time."

Noelle explained what she thought they should do, and the girls loved her idea.

"OMG, you're freaking brilliant," Micah said.

They started by shoveling the snow that was piled up against the curb and on the steps in front of the school, then moved on to shoveling more snow from the grass and whatever was left on the sidewalk.

"You know, if our school was in any other neighborhood, this prank wouldn't even be possible," Lux said sourly. "Like my dad's neighborhood. There wasn't any snow even left in front of our bougie building."

"Yeah," Noelle agreed. "But the city seems to

forget to salt and plow areas where people like us live."

"Well, it's working in our favor today," Tobyn said with a grin.

They piled the snow, little by little, up against the doors of the school from the ground to the top of the doorframe. They packed it tight and high, then rounded out the sides, top, and bottom as best they could into the shape of a giant butterfly. The snow blocked the doors completely, and then they used the packets of Kool-Aid to stain the snow butterfly's wings in bright splashes of color.

When they'd finished, they stepped back to admire their work. It looked beautiful, but more importantly, it would be a huge pain for anyone to get into the school building that morning.

"Yaaaaaas!" Tobyn shouted. She wrapped her arm around Noelle's shoulders. Then Lux threw her arm over Tobyn's, and Micah came over and leaned against Lux, completing the pile. They were a mess of friendship and accomplishment, and they were all grinning, mouths wide.

"This is good," Micah said.

"Damn good," Lux agreed. She pulled out her phone and snapped a photo, and Noelle tried hard to smile and laugh with her friends. It was a great prank, it had been her idea, and they'd actually pulled it off. But all she could think about was how close she stood to Tobyn, and how the butterfly on the door was nothing compared to the butterflies in her stomach.

A few hours later, when the girls returned to school, trying their best to look innocent and surprised, the block was packed with students. Everyone crowded around the doors trying to take photos of the snow butterfly even as the janitor chipped away at the bottom.

"Go slow," one teacher said, "you don't want to damage the door."

"I think I got it," the janitor said, rolling his eyes.

Lux pushed her lips together to hold in her smile.

Micah coughed, to hide her laugh.

Tobyn turned and covered her mouth with her hand.

Noelle, who had the best poker face of the bunch, pulled out her phone, looking bored.

Emmett, Lux's crush, walked over and stood with them. He whispered, "The Flyy Girls strike again." Lux punched him in the arm.

Noelle glared at him for a split second. But then, she couldn't help it. Even she smirked.